The
Three Little
Princesses

Brooke

Tan-tan-terrah!

Look out for more storybooks by
Georgie Adams and Emily Bolam . . .

The Three Little Pirates
The Three Little Witches

The Three Little Princesses

Georgie Adams and Emily Bolam

Orion
Children's Books

First published in Great Britain in 2007
by Orion Children's Books
This edition first published in Great Britain in 2010
by Orion Children's Books
a division of the Orion Publishing Group Ltd
Orion House
5 Upper St Martin's Lane
London WC2H 9EA
An Hachette UK Company

7 9 10 8 6

ISBN 978 1 84255 633 7

Printed in China

The Orion Publishing Group's policy is to use papers that are natural,
renewable and recyclable products made from wood grown in sustainable forests.
The logging and manufacturing processes are expected to conform
to the environmental regulations of the country of origin.

www.orionbooks.co.uk

5

For my good eggs Abby and Imogen,
with love, as ever
G.A.

Contents

Chapter 1

Here Come the Princesses!

. . . Tan-tan-terrah! Tan-tan-terrah!

Ladies and gentlemen! Boys and girls!
Introducing their royal highnesses,

Princess
Phoebe . . .

Princess
Pruella . . .

. . . and
Princess Pip!

12

The three little princesses live in Pepperpot Palace with their parents, the king and queen.

The three little princesses each have their own room . . .

Here's my room. And this is my favourite dress!

The Bean Stalks

Princess Phoebe

14

My room next!
I'm pony-mad,
as you can
see!

My room's
a bit messy,
but I like it
that way!

16

The three little princesses each have their own pony. They love riding whenever they can.

But it's not *all* fun being a princess!
Every day Phoebe, Pruella and Pip have to
learn how to be proper little princesses.
Their teacher, Madame Rum-ba-ba, teaches
them how to curtsey . . .

. . . wave from
a golden coach

. . . and eat dainty cakes at garden parties!

This is their school timetable:

Monday	Letter Writing	Playtime	Looking at Magic Mirrors
Tuesday	How to Make a Speech	Playtime	Garden Parties
Wednesday	Smiling and Waving	Playtime	Polite Conversation
Thursday	Walking gracefully	Playtime	Ballroom Dancing
Friday	Greeting People	Playtime	Dresses, shoes and tiaras

And now,
by royal command from
their Royal Highnesses . . .
ON WITH THE STORY!

Chapter 2
Madame Rum-ba-ba and the Funky Frogs

It was breakfast time at Pepperpot Palace and the three little princesses were hurrying down to the dining hall. On the way Phoebe, Pruella and Pip passed Toby the time machine.

TEN PAST EIGHT.
TICK, TOCK, TUT!
LATE AGAIN!

The little princesses raced into the dining hall. After saying good morning to their mum and dad, they tucked into their bowls of Posh Pops.

"What lessons have we got today?" asked Pip.

Phoebe put down her silver spoon and opened her diary. "It's Thursday," she said. "Walking gracefully and ballroom dancing."

I'd much rather be riding!

"Cheer up! It's my birthday in two days' time," said the king.

"There will be a gymkhana in the afternoon, and a fancy-dress ball in the evening!"

Then the king took a large golden key from his pocket. "I must go and wind Toby," he said.

The queen, who was sitting far away, didn't hear properly. "What was that?" she asked.

"Dad has to wind Toby!" yelled Phoebe.

"And he's got the only key," added Pip.

"Ah!" said the queen vaguely.

After breakfast, the princesses hurried along to the schoolroom.

"Good morning, your royal highnesses,"
said Madame Rum-ba-ba. "Today we will
practise walking gracefully, wearing your tiara
at *just* the right angle."

For this lesson they had to parade in front
of Millicént, the magic mirror.

"I hope Millicent is in a good mood
today," whispered Phoebe.

25

When all three little princesses managed to wear their tiaras correctly, Madame Rum-ba-ba gave them each a smiley star.

RIGHT!

WRONG!

HOPELESS!

At breaktime Phoebe, Pruella and Pip chatted about the king's birthday party.

The fancy-dress ball will be such fun! But what are we going to wear?

We've got to buy our costumes AND get ready for the gymkhana.

Oh, beanstalks! There's so much to do!

"There will be no lessons tomorrow morning," said Madame Rum-ba-ba. "Instead you may go to Goblin Market to buy your costumes. But you must be back in time for an important test in the afternoon."

"What test?" asked Phoebe, puzzled.

"Wait and see," said Madame Rum-ba-ba. "*Now* it's time for ballroom dancing!"

Today Madame Rum-ba-ba had a surprise in store. She beamed at the princesses.

"I have arranged for some handsome young princes to join us," she said, beckoning to three boys, cowering behind some chairs. Phoebe, Pruella and Pip were horrified.

Madame Rum-ba-ba told everyone
to choose a partner and dance around
the ballroom.

"One, two, three . . .
one, two, three!"

While they were dancing, Horace, Edwin and Nigel told the little princesses they were pretty fed up.

"We've got a band," said Horace.

"We're The Funky Frogs," said Edwin.

"We'd rather be doing that than prancing around here," said Nigel.

"A band!" exclaimed Phoebe. "That's so cool!"

"You could play at the fancy-dress ball!" said Pip.

They all agreed it was a brilliant idea.

Suddenly, Horace, Edwin and Nigel
stopped ballroom dancing and started . . .
BREAKDANCING!

The little princesses couldn't resist joining
in and they all ended up in a tangled heap!

Funky!

Great
beat!

Cool!

Chapter 3

Prancing Ponies and Princess Priscilla

That afternoon the three little princesses practised for the gymkhana.

Florence, Barley and Star were frisky and eager to get going!

The princesses rode them into the field and decided what to do first.

"Jumping," said Pruella.

34

Afterwards they played a game
of stepping stones.

Oh, bogbeans!
Here comes
Princess Perfect.

Princess Priscilla, the
snooty princess from the
kingdom next-door, had
arrived. She was riding her
new pony, Topaz.

"I shall be riding Topaz in the gymkhana," Princess Priscilla began grandly.

Then, because she had just lost her front tooth, Priscilla finished with a lisp. "You don't *thtand a chanth* on those old ponith! I'm coming to the *fanthy-dreth* ball too," she went on. "My *cothtume* will be the *betht!*"

And she trotted off, leaving the princesses hopping mad.

The princesses rode Florence, Barley and Star back to the stables.

They gave their ponies plenty to eat, and put them to bed.

Then they skipped and sang all the way
back to the palace.

To go shop, shop,
shopping.

We're hop,
hop, hopping!

Without stop, stop,
stopping!

Hooray!

38

Chapter 4
Gossip, Goblins and a Wish!

Early next morning, Phoebe, Pruella and Pip woke to the sounds of shouting. Guards were running up and down the corridors.

That morning as the little princesses' maids, Clarissa, Maisy and Alice, helped their royal charges to dress, they told the little princesses what had happened.

"The key to Toby the time machine has gone missing," said Clarissa.

"If Toby stops," said Alice, "the kingdom and everyone in it will *disappear* in a puff of smoke!"

The three little princesses gasped.
This was *terrible*! What *could* they do?

But right now, they decided to go to
Goblin Market, as planned.

On their way out, the princesses stopped
to look at Toby. He was singing!

HICKORY, DICKORY, DOCK –
THE MOUSE RAN UP THE CLOCK . . .

Look! There
are only ten
hours left.

Come on.
There's no
time
to lose!

How weird.
He's never
done THAT
before!

Goblin Market was just outside the palace walls — not far from the Enchanted Forest, a dangerous and magical place where the princesses had been forbidden ever to go.

There was so much to see and do!

"Let's split up and do our own shopping," said Phoebe. "We can meet up later at the tea shop."

Phoebe went to buy some new shoes. She had decided to go to the fancy-dress ball as Cinderella, and was hoping to find a pair of glass slippers.

The elf shoemaker measured Phoebe's feet and made the daintiest pair of glass slippers you have ever seen. They fitted perfectly!

Meanwhile, Pruella met Horace, Edwin and Nigel who were out shopping too. The Funky Frogs had just bought themselves new guitars.

Suddenly, Pruella spotted someone hurrying towards them.

It was Princess Priscilla! "Cooeee, boys!
Oh, my shopping is *so* heavy!" she sighed.
"I *thuppose* you couldn't
help a *damthel* in *dithtweth?*"

Oh no!

Let's go.

Too
late . . .

She's
seen us!

Helping a damsel in distress was the last
thing Horace, Edwin and Nigel had on their
minds. But they were much too nice to say so.

47

As soon as they had gone, Pruella hurried into a shop to look for her costume.

With the help of the goblin assistant, she found exactly what she wanted. "That one, please," Pruella said, pointing to a Little Red Riding Hood outfit.

48

Pip was going to the fancy-dress ball as a fairy queen. But she just *couldn't* decide which crown to wear!

Some helpful assistants brought her boxes and boxes of glittering jewels to choose from until . . .

Just then, a real fairy popped into the shop. It was the good fairy, Isadora.

"You'll need a wand," said Isadora in a business-like way. "Every fairy queen must have a wand!"

Isadora snapped her fingers and a silver wand appeared, like magic.

PING!

"And I'll grant you a wish," said Isadora. "I've got time for just one. But don't take all day about it!"

So, Pip closed her eyes tight, took a deep breath and . . . WISHED.

I WISH I knew where Toby's key was!

"Hm!" said Isadora. "Tricky, that one. Let me see . . . a goblin with no name has it. You'll find him in the Enchanted Forest. But take care! The wicked witch Gondola lives there. Good luck and look after that wand!"

Then she vanished.

POOF!

Just like that.

So when Phoebe, Pruella and Pip met up at the The Crooked House Tea Shop, they had lots to talk about!

The three little princesses made up their minds. To look for the goblin with no name, they would have to be very, *very* brave and . . . go into the Enchanted Forest!

Chapter 5
The Mysterious Test

Phoebe, Pruella and Pip raced back to the palace to leave their shopping.

On the way to their rooms, they went to see Toby. He shouted, in a slowed-down, wonky voice.

TEST TIME WITH MADAME RUMBLE . . . BUMBLE . . . BUM!

"Oh, bogbeans!" exclaimed Phoebe, remembering. "We've got that mystery test with Madame Rum-ba-ba this afternoon!"

The princesses had forgotten all about it.

Madame Rum-ba-ba explained the test. It was hard to concentrate when there was such an important task ahead of them.

"You must each *kiss* one of these dear little FROGS, and turn it into a prince! Now, pick up your frogs and begin!" said Madame Rum-ba-ba.

The three little princesses had no choice.
So they . . .

held their noses . . .

closed their eyes . . .

plucked up
courage and . . .

KISSED THEM!

The princesses' first attempts were not entirely successful.

But eventually they got it right!

Then the princesses ran to change into their riding clothes. As Pip was pulling on her jacket, she caught sight of the silver wand Isadora had given her and grabbed it.

On their way out of the palace, the princesses heard Toby singing a strange, sad little song:

ONE O'CLOCK,
TWO O'CLOCK,
THREE O'CLOCK,
FOUR.
FIVE O'CLOCK,
SIX O'CLOCK . . .
HOW MANY MORE?

Then they dashed to the stables. Phoebe, Pruella and Pip saddled up their ponies as quickly as they could. They had only six hours to search for the goblin with no name and find the key.

Chapter 6
The Enchanted Forest

The Enchanted Forest was a dark and forbidding place! The trees were enormous and some looked very frightening.

After a while they came to a signpost.

Which way?

They both look gloomy.

Suddenly, Florence, Barley and Star set off down the path towards Apple Wood. It was as if something or someone was telling them what to do. How strange!

In no time they found themselves in a wood full of big red, rosy apples. The apples looked delicious! So Phoebe, Pruella and Pip jumped off their ponies and picked some.

And they each took ONE . . . BIG . . . BITE!

Yummy!

Apples!

Mmmm!

Little did they know that the wicked witch Gondola had put a sleepy spell on those apples. No sooner had everyone taken a bite, than they all fell fast asleep.

And all the while the wicked witch had been watching them.

Gondola rubbed her hands together happily. "Well, my sleeping beauties, that should delay you from finding the goblin. I need *him* to make a potion!"

And with that, the witch flew off on her broomstick.

Pip hadn't been asleep for long when she felt something sharp sticking into her. It woke her up.

"Ouch!" she cried.

Pip looked in her jacket pocket and
found Isadora's silver wand.

Lucky I remembered to bring it! she
thought. I wonder if it can do magic?

Then she waved the wand over Phoebe,
Pruella and the ponies and said, "Wake up!"

"Wha —
what happened?"
said Phoebe.

"I had a strange
dream," said Pruella,
rubbing her eyes.

"We must have been
under a bad spell," said
Pip. "Isadora warned us
about the wicked witch Gondola.
This is all her doing!"

The little princesses were no nearer to
finding the goblin, and time was ticking
away . . .

Back at Pepperpot Palace everyone
looked very worried. There were only three
hours left!

If the key couldn't be found . . . if Toby
couldn't be wound . . .

Everyone was so busy that they hadn't
noticed the princesses were missing.

"Let's go back and try the other path," said Phoebe. "The one that goes to Silver Fish Lake."

The princesses got on their ponies and trotted back along the path. But it seemed much longer than before!

"How strange," said Phoebe. "We should
have reached the signpost by now."

"I'm sure that tree moved!" said Pruella.

"Oh, not another spell!" moaned Pip.

At last — there it was. This time it spoke.

"That way!" said the signpost, pointing to Silver Fish Lake. "I could have told you the right way the first time you were here, but you didn't ask."

"Well, really . . . !" Phoebe began.

But Pruella said: "There's no time to argue. Come on, let's go!"

Soon, the three little princesses saw Silver Fish Lake through the trees. No sooner had they reached the water's edge when a shiny silver fish popped up!

"We *wish* to find the goblin with no name," said Pruella.

In less than a wink the fish replied, "You'll find him at the end of the rainbow."

The fish swam away, leaving behind seven colourful bubbles. The seven bubbles floated into the sky to make a magical — *rainbow!*

Chapter 7
The Curse of the Goblin with No Name

The wicked witch Gondola sat in another part of the Enchanted Forest. She stirred a cauldron and sniffed a smelly brew.

Not long now. One more thing to add and my potion will be ready!

The unlucky thing was, at that moment, hiding under a toadstool. It was a goblin — the very goblin the little princesses were looking for.

Hello!
Yes, it's me.
The goblin
with no name!

I was on my way to work at Pepperpot Palace when I tripped over Gondola's broomstick.

Before I could say sorry, Gondola flew into a rage and put a curse on me!

You will forget
your name! If in
TWO days you
cannot remember
it, I'll BOIL
you in a potion!

So I stole Toby's key
to stop the time
machine. I thought
if it stopped time
would stand still,
and give me more
time to think of
my name.

I've been thinking
and thinking
but I just can't
remember my name!

Was it Fleabee? Wiggletoes?
Squill . . .?

The goblin was *still* thinking when a beautiful rainbow appeared. Then, to his surprise, he saw the three little princesses galloping towards him! Phoebe, Pruella and Pip recognised the goblin at once. He was one of the king's servants!

At first they were very angry with him.

Quickly the goblin told them about the witch's curse, and how he thought that stealing the key would help him.

"Oh no!" cried Phoebe. "If Toby stops, the kingdom and everyone in it will *disappear!*"

"Including *you!*" said Pruella.

"So please, GIVE US THE KEY!" said Pip.

The goblin said, "You can have the key on one condition. You must tell me . . . MY NAME!"

The princesses could hardly believe their ears.

There are
HUNDREDS!

Guess
your name?
You must be
joking!

We'll never
get it right!

But there was nothing they could do
or say to change his mind. Everything and
everyone depended on them now. They *had*
to guess the goblin's name!

Longnose?
Frogbit?
Gobbler?
Bristlebeard?
Snippet?
Sneezel?
Bandylegs?
Wormwood?
Teaseyweed?
Witloof?
Sickelbur?
Catchfly?
Goosefoot?
Rumpus?
Pepperwort?

NO!
TRY AGAIN!
WRONG!

In desperation, Phoebe cried, "Oh, bogbeans! We'll never get it right!"

The goblin leaped up. "BOGBEANS! That's it!"

Then the goblin and the little princesses all danced around and sang for joy.

And somewhere on the far side of the forest, Gondola heard the rumpus! She was furious. In her temper the wicked witch kicked over the cauldron, spilling every drop of that disgusting potion.

Bogbeans is his name, Bogbeans is his name. Hey, ho, now we know, BOGBEANS is his name!

Aaaaaah!
The curse
is broken.

Chapter 8

Time for Fun and Fancy-Dress!

The moon shone clear and bright that night over Pepperpot Palace, but everything inside seemed gloomy.

Everyone had searched high and low for the key. But it could not be found.

As they waited for whatever was to happen, the maids looked around.

It was then they noticed that Phoebe, Pruella and Pip were not there.

Suddenly, they were all startled as —
BANG! — the palace gates flew open and in
burst . . . the three little princesses!

"We've got the key, Dad!" shouted Phoebe.

"Quick!" cried Pruella. "Let's wind Toby together."

And so they did. In no time, Toby's cogs and wheels were whirring again, and all was well.

The kingdom had been saved!

Hip, hip, hip, hooray!

Next day was the king's birthday!
The three little princesses were up bright
and early. There was so much to tell their
parents, they all talked at once!

The king forgave Bogbeans. And to
show how much he trusted him, the king
made him — Keeper of the Key! Bogbeans
was very proud.

That afternoon, a big crowd gathered to watch the gymkhana. Everyone had heard about the little princesses' daring adventures. So, when they came into the ring, the crowd cheered and cheered.

The first event was jumping and although Florence, Barley and Star did their best — they made a few mistakes!

Princess Priscilla and Topaz jumped everything perfectly. She won First Prize.

But Phoebe, Pruella and Pip each won events with their ponies in . . .

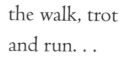
the walk, trot and run. . .

the balloon race and . . .

musical mats!

So everyone was happy!

That evening, the ballroom twinkled with fairy lights. The little princesses had great fun putting on their costumes.

Things didn't go *quite* to plan
when Phoebe borrowed Pip's wand.
"I wonder if it can turn this pumpkin
into a coach?" she said, waving it about.

But the pumpkin turned into a
gigantic . . .

HOT-AIR BALLOON!

Priscilla, dressed as a Purrfect White Cat,
was standing nearby. She was whisked
away in the basket!

WhOOOOOOOmph

Luckily, the good fairy Isadora arrived
just in time to put things right.

Later, it was the fancy-dress ball. Horace, Edwin and Nigel played their new guitars and everyone, even Madame Rum-ba-ba, rocked and rolled.

Phoebe, Pruella and Pip danced until
they thought their feet would drop off!

But all too soon it was time to go. When Toby called out, "MIDNIGHT!" everyone went home to bed.

So now it's time for us to say . . .

"Goodnight Phoebe."

"Goodnight Pip."

"Goodnight Pruella."

Goodnight, little princesses.
Goodnight!